Ꝺellie Ꝺova's

Summer on the Run

By: Stephenie Peterson

Ella.

Always remember you can change the world.

Jd   Au

Illustrations by: Jo Painter

DEDICATION

In memory of Ann Wilson.

"What we have once enjoyed deeply we can never
lose. All that we love deeply becomes a part of us."
–Helen Keller

ACKNOWLEDGMENTS

Deborah Emans was my high school drama teacher. I was lucky to know her then, and even luckier now. Thank you, Debbie, for your help with this book. You made all the difference.

Michelle Ristuccia, thank you so much for your assistance with this project. Having the perspective of a fellow author has been so helpful.

My parents always have been supportive of my creative endeavors. Thank you for not trying to convince me to be practical. What a waste that would have been.

My kids have become my biggest cheerleaders.

Keagan, Eden, and Aviel, thank you so much for supporting me and for being patient with me when I am busy working.

My husband has been so encouraging of my work. Thank you, Nick, for understanding my need to get these stories out there and for moving mountains to make it work for our family.

While I was working on this book, my grandmother passed away. Ann Wilson inspired me every day of her life and continues to do so in the afterlife. Thank you, Grandma. You made me who I am today.

To my readers, thank you so much for your support. Your feedback has been so encouraging. Your emails and book reviews have ensured that I will keep writing. Thank you!

CHAPTER ONE

Terror encompassed Nellie Nova's entire being. She looked around, trying to comprehend what had happened. Only moments before, she'd been having a pleasant conversation with a delightful group of people about their travels across America. In an instant, she and her companions were surrounded by a pack of snarling wolves. She looked to her brother, Niles for help, but his fear-filled eyes told her that he didn't have any more answers than she did.

The Nova kids used their time machine to travel back in time to meet one of Nellie's heroes, Saca-gawea, and the men she traveled with. If you know anything about the Nova kids, you know that they are extraordinarily brave kids. They've seen things you and I could only ever imagine. It took a lot to

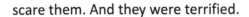

scare them. And they were terrified.

Nellie tried to slow her rapid breathing. She was fairly certain that you were not supposed to let wild animals sense your fear. She was not sure how she knew this. Maybe she'd read something about fear and animals in a book? Her mind started to wander to the source of this information for a moment, but then she snapped back to the horrible reality before her.

She turned to the men to her left. Meriweather Lewis looked almost as afraid as Niles did. William Clark looked at his feet. Toussaint Charbonneau looked toward his wife for answers. Nellie turned her head slightly to see what she thought they should do next.

The young Native American mother wore her baby on her back. Her face was serious as she spoke quietly, though only her husband could understand the language she used. Despite the fact that Sacagawea did not speak English, the entire group seemed to calm a bit when she spoke. She held up her hand to indicate that no one should move. Then she pointed behind them and took a slow, measured step backward. She nodded and the rest of the group followed suit.

The wolves stood still as the group backed away. Sacagawea headed slowly toward her camp. Her baby let out a small whimper and she quietly hushed the child. She avoided turning her back to the wolves. Each member of the party did the same. Nellie and Niles carefully copied their movements.

They had made it to the edge of the camp when something quite horrible happened. Niles, in his rush to get away from the terrifying canines, was not looking where he walked. His foot caught a large gnarled tree root and he tripped and stumbled to the ground. A wolf lunged forward and gnashed its teeth aggressively at him as he tried to get back on his feet.

Clark grabbed Niles' hand and pulled him up, but it was too late. The wolves saw Niles as weak and several lunged at him. Clark whisked him onto his shoulders. Niles looked as though he might vomit from fear. Sacagawea turned toward the fire at the camp and stuck a piece of firewood into the flames. She pulled it out and shouted at the wolves, waving the flaming branch toward them. She nodded to the men and they did the same. Nellie joined in as well. Her heartbeat pounded in

her ears. She'd never been so frightened in her life. The air was filled with the wolves' growls and the shouts of the group of travelers. After a few terrifying minutes, the wolves turned around and ran away. Relief swept over the camp.

Sacagawea had saved them all.

Once everyone calmed down, the Nellie and Niles decided that it was time to leave 1805. The kids started their goodbyes. When they spoke their thanks to Sacagawea, they had do so through a chain of translators, but her eyes and smile told them she understood the sentiment behind their words long before she was told their meaning. She nodded to the kids, who waved goodbye and headed back into the woods. Back to their time machine. Back to their own time.

Nellie and Niles chatted about their experiences with Sacagawea as they walked toward the time machine. Nellie felt a rush of adrenaline. How lucky was she to have met the famous Native American trail guide who helped Lewis and Clark on their expedition to the Pacific?

"I can't believe how brave she was with the wolves!" Niles told his sister.

"I know! But it makes sense. I mean she was brave enough to go on that trip to start with. Can you imagine? Walking across America with a baby on your back?" Nellie answered.

"I can't. That *is* brave!" Niles shook his head, marveling at Sacagawea's courage.

They'd reached their time machine, hidden well within the trees. It's mirrored invisibility shield made it difficult to spot.

"Hello Purple Flyer," Nellie said. "Turn off the invisibility shield."

"Hello, Nellie Nova. Invisibility shield disarmed," a computerized voice chirped back, and the machine's windows and purple walls became visible as a series of mirrors turned.

Niles opened the door and held it for his sister. They entered the machine and closed the door. Nellie spoke again, "Take us home, Purple Flyer!"

A green light filled the time machine and it began to spin wildly. The machine lifted off the ground and they began their spiraling journey through eternity toward their home.

CHAPTER TWO

Nellie and Niles landed safely, albeit shakily, in their tree house in 2016. They scrambled down the ladder and made a beeline for the house to tell their parents all about their adventures with Sacagawea. After several minutes of excited discussion, Nellie went to her room and pulled out a journal. The inside of the book was filled with her notes about visits to the past. She flipped past entries about meeting Maya Angelou, Princess Diana, and Florence Nightingale and started a new entry about their brief, but action-packed meeting with Sacagawea. Nellie's most exceptional mind kicked into overdrive as she wrote.

I must tell you that man has not invented words

that truly describe the wonder that lives inside Nellie's mind, but I will try my best to relay the immense treasure that is hidden within. Inside Nellie's mind exists a hall of amazement. Books taller than grown men stood in one corner flipping their gilded pages in rapid succession. A symphony of invisible musicians composed itself, instruments floating in midair and created a soundtrack to their adventure with Sacagawea. Tropical birds with colorful feathers swooped past dancing ballerinas as a wall of gears seemed to mimic the dancers' movements behind them. Nellie found time travel exhilarating and she thoroughly enjoyed journaling about it.

Just as she closed her purple leather journal, Niles knocked on her door. She stood and opened it.

"Want to go visit James and Ruby?" he asked.

James and Ruby were friends from another time. The Nova kids had met the orphaned siblings in Victorian London while they were on their first journey in time. When they met 1930s navigator Fred Noonan, they knew these three people belonged together. Nellie and Niles rescued Fred and Amelia Earhart by landing The Purple Flyer on Amelia's plane the day they went missing in 1937 and brought the aviators home with them. Fred was lonely after being forced to move his life to 2015. Thanks to the Nova kids, James, Ruby and Fred were happily living in a small English village in the 1960s.

"Did you check with Mom?" Nellie asked her brother. While they enjoyed a lot of freedom for kids their age, the Nova family had one very important rule. The kids were not supposed to travel time without permission.

"Yup. We're cleared for takeoff," Niles answered with a smile.

Nellie rushed toward her bedroom door. The Nova kids didn't usually take multiple time traveling adventures in a day, but she wasn't about to turn down a chance to visit her friends.

"Let's go!" she called to her brother as she pushed by him.

The kids chorused cheerful goodbyes to their mother as they headed out the door and into the jungle-like backyard. As they climbed the ladder to the tree house, they discussed when in time they should arrive at their friends' home. They decided the visit about a year after they'd last seen Fred, James and Ruby.

They left the machine in the yard they knew to belong to James, Ruby, and Fred. They'd visited twice before to check in with their friends.

Nellie and Niles walked excitedly to the front door and knocked. Fred opened the door, and upon seeing them, smiled broadly.

"Niles! Nellie! So good to see you! How was your trip?" Both his facial expression and his warm voice let them know that Fred was happy to have unexpected company.

"It was great! I love time travel!" Niles answered.

"Sit down," he told them, pointing to a cozy living room. "I'll get Ruby and James."

A moment later, they heard a squeal of excitement from the other room and the pitter-patter of running feet. James and Ruby appeared in the doorway.

"Nellie! Niles! It's oh so good to see you. Thanks ever so much for coming." Ruby said.

"Hi! Thanks for coming!" James added.

They sat on the sofa and talked about how Ruby, James, and Fred were adjusting to their new time. They all seemed very happy. Ruby and James had made a lot of friends at school and Fred had taken a job as a mechanic.

Nellie was so glad to see the three of them living a lovely life together. They'd all been a bit lost when the Nova kids first encountered them.

It is such a relief that the kids didn't have to worry about where they'll get food and that Fred isn't lonely anymore, Nellie thought, remembering how difficult life used to be for her friends.

The Nova kids stayed for a dinner of roast chicken and potatoes. The group of friends chatted and laughed and soon it was time for James and Ruby to head to bed and Nellie and Niles to head home. Of course, the Nova kids didn't leave before giving lots and lots of hugs and promising to visit again soon.

Nellie and Niles walked back to the Purple Flyer and ordered it to take them to their own time. They braced themselves for the incredible journey through time. They began to twirl around and around. Green light surrounded them. The machine lifted up and suddenly they were spinning through eternity. Out one window, Nellie saw children dressed in the clothes of early American pioneers running through a field and in the same moment,

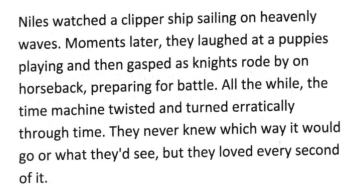

Niles watched a clipper ship sailing on heavenly waves. Moments later, they laughed at a puppies playing and then gasped as knights rode by on horseback, preparing for battle. All the while, the time machine twisted and turned erratically through time. They never knew which way it would go or what they'd see, but they loved every second of it.

Nellie noticed that their yard was now visible below them.

"Get ready!" she told her brother. They braced for a rough landing. Even though they'd added tires to the bottom of the time machine to act as bumpers, landings in the Purple Flyer were never as smooth as one would hope.

After their jarring landing, the kids got out of the time machine and headed inside to check in with their mother. They updated Annie on how every- one was doing and headed back outside.

"You up for a walk around the neighborhood?" Nellie asked Niles.

"Sure," he replied. Time travel had brought the Nova siblings closer together. They hardly ever argued anymore. Well, maybe "hardly ever argued" is a bit of a stretch. They were siblings after all, and siblings are known for quarreling. Generally, however, Nellie and Niles quite enjoyed one another's company these days.

They called goodbye to their mom and made their way down their driveway and onto their twisty, peaceful street. They chatted excitedly about the happenings of the day. They walked for about twenty minutes, enjoying the sunshine and conversation.

A car drove by and neither child paid any attention to it. Oh, how I wish they did see it. Or maybe that it never drove by to begin with. But the car driving by is an important part of our story and without it, well, it would be a different story all together. Unfortunately, the black car did drive by without either of the Nova kids noticing it at all. They went along their way as if nothing had happened.

Niles pointed to the park nearby and suggested they reroute their stroll along the walking path. Nellie nodded in agreement and they headed in the direction of the path. As they started down the trail, she heard a car door shut and looked behind her.

A sinking feeling rushed over her as she took notice

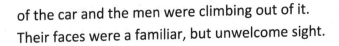
of the car and the men were climbing out of it. Their faces were a familiar, but unwelcome sight.

"Niles!" she hissed. "It's Riley and his cronies!"

Niles stopped and slowly turned around. Once he saw them, he yelled "Run!"

And run they did. They sprinted through the park as fast as they could. They headed for a wooded area so that they would be harder to spot. The agents, who were fairly far behind them to start with, had a hard time keeping up. The kids reached the end of the park and they could hear the men struggling through some bushes. They kept running, down the street, past the bank, past the butcher shop, past the police station.

Niles looked over his shoulder and saw that the agents lagged behind them. He pulled Nellie's hand and they turned a corner, then another, then one more. They found themselves standing in front of the library and ran up the many stairs of the old building, looked around once so they could be sure the agents weren't watching, and ducked inside. Panting, Nellie whispered to her brother (naturally as one does not shout in a library, even if they are being chased) "Do you think we will be safe here?"

Niles nodded. "I don't think they know which way we went anymore."

Nellie breathed in the familiar, booky smell of the library. She certainly felt safer here than she did outside.

"Okay," she whispered to Niles, "But we should at least head to the back of the building."

Niles nodded and they walked aimlessly through the building. Nellie ran her right index finger along the spines of a row of books as they made their way as far from the entrance as they could. They reached the back of the library. To their right was the bathroom and to their left was a staircase. They decided to head down the stairs, assuming that if the agents did come into the large, maze-like building, they probably would not search it thoroughly and getting off the main floor would only help to hide them.

The Nova kids tried very hard to appear calm. As frightened as they were, but they still didn't want to be easy to spot if the agents decided to search for them in the library. I also have to tell you, that they were trying very hard to fool themselves. Deep down, they were terrified, but they did not want to admit it. After all of their adventures, they

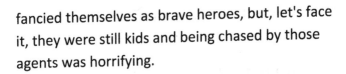

fancied themselves as brave heroes, but, let's face it, they were still kids and being chased by those agents was horrifying.

"I don't get it," Niles finally said, after they'd wandered silently for 15 minutes or so. "They've left us alone for so long. Why come back now?"

"I don't know," said Nellie, quietly. "But I don't like it."

Just then, a man in a black suit rounded a corner. Nellie let out a gasp and backed into a shelf, knocking several books off of it with a thud. The man, not an agent, but a friendly businessman searching for a good novel, gave the kids a confused look and asked,

"You okay?"

The Nova kids nodded and bent over to pick up the mess. The man smiled at the kids and returned to his quest to find the perfect book. Nellie scooped up an armful of books and realized they were all biographies.

"Oh, I just love biographies," she told her brother, who was struggling with a pile of books himself.

Nellie placed a book about Lucile Ball back on the shelf. Niles scanned the bookcase looking for the proper place for the book about Larry Bird he had in his hand. It appeared that they had disassembled most of the "B" section, so it took a while to get everything back in order.

They finished up and started to walk away when they noticed one last book that had flown further than the others. Nellie leaned down to get it and noticed the title. "A Biography of Nellie Bly."

"Niles look, she has my name!" Nellie whispered excitedly and she sat down on the floor and started skimming the book.

Nellie lost herself in her reading about Ms. Bly, who turned out to be utterly fascinating. Nellie was so impressed by the actions of the spunky reporter from the late 1800s that she could not put down

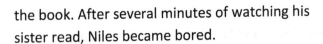

the book. After several minutes of watching his sister read, Niles became bored.

"Hey, read about your namesake later," he told her. "We really should be getting home to tell Mom and Dad what is going on."

Nellie begrudgingly agreed. She quickly checked out the book (Nellie Nova never left home without her library card) and they headed for the exit.

They made their way home through alleyways, fields, and the park, hoping that they could avoid crossing paths with the agents again. Niles was still on edge, but Nellie's mind had moved on past the agents. Nellie was too excited to be scared. All she could think about was getting home to read more about Nellie Bly.

CHAPTER THREE

A lot had changed in the year since Nellie built her time machine, The Purple Flyer. Life has a way of rearranging itself as time passes. For one, Amelia Earhart was a permanent resident of the house the Nova family playfully named Casa Nova. Amelia returned home with Nellie and Niles last year and never left. At first, the plan was to help her get used to living in 2015, however, she soon was a part of the family. Amelia went back to flight school to get licensed as a professional pilot and started flying commercial airplanes for a national airline. "Auntie Amelia" was gone frequently, but the Novas all loved having her as part of the family.

Nellie and Niles traveled in time as often as their

parents, Fox and Annie, would allow. Nellie still had a long list of amazing women she wanted to meet and introduce to Niles, who spurred her desire to create a time machine when he told her no woman had ever changed the world. Niles, who continued to tease his sister (he was, after all, still a big brother) never really believed his own words, but now, that he and Nellie had met several world-changing women, he knew for a fact that women around the globe had changed the world for the better.

Fox still worked part-time at the local university and conducted physics research at home. Inspired by his daughter's scientific achievement of building a time machine, his physics experiments were bigger and better than ever. The Nova home could get quite rambunctious with all of his projects, but the science-loving family thrived when surrounded by chaos.

Annie recently made a major discovery at the research lab where she worked as a botanist. She'd even been on the cover of *Women of Science* magazine. It made the whole family nervous to have reporters out to the house. They worried about someone finding the time machine, but everything had gone smoothly. The story was a hit and made no mention of the Nova family's adven-

tures in time travel.

Nellie and Niles stayed busy with their home-schooling, dance lessons, Girl Scouts, church activities, art classes, and soccer practices, but they made sure to make room in their schedule for time traveling. They frequently convinced their parents to let them use the time machine when they pointed out how much it helped their history studies.

It truly had been an amazing year for the Nova family. Nellie, who would soon turn ten, could hardly believe all of it. Some days she worried that it had all been a wonderful dream, but it was all very real. Only, now, with the agents from the National Agency for Technology and Air Travel (N.A.T.) after them again, it started to feel like a nightmare.

The kids threw open the door to Casa Nova and ran through the house until they bumped into Annie, who carried a tray of seedlings towards the back door. Niles' elbow slammed the tray and it went flying, sending dirt and tiny plants all over the kitchen. Soil and seeds covered the room, creating a spectacular mess from the tile floor to the burners on the stove-top.

"Niles! Nellie! What is going on here? You know

better than to run in the house!" Annie scolded. She softened when she noticed the look on the kids' faces. "What's wrong?" Her eyes reflected her children's fear.

"We saw them, Mom," panted Niles. "The agents."

"They chased us through town," Nellie added.

"We hid in the library," Niles told her.

Annie shook her head and sat down at the kitchen table, forgetting about the mess that still needed to be cleaned. Amelia walked into the room. Her eyes widened at the sight of the disastrous state of the kitchen.

"What happened in here? Do you kiddos need my help cleaning up?" She asked.

"They're back, Amelia," Annie told her.

"Who's back?" Amelia's voice showed her concern.

"Riley and his men. They're back and they chased the kids all over town," Annie fretted.
Amelia took the seat next to Annie and shook her head in disbelief.

"What are we going to do?" she asked.

No one had an answer.

Ten minutes later, the front door opened and in Fox walked into the house whistling cheerfully. When he entered the kitchen to find the group sitting silently around the kitchen table, his whistling abruptly stopped. The combination of the dirt scattered all over the room and the expressions on everyone's faces instantly worried him. Before he could open his mouth to ask what was wrong, Annie spoke.

"The agents are back. They chased the kids through town earlier this afternoon."

Fox's heart sank. They'd had almost a year of peace since Nellie tricked the agents into thinking that all they had was a toy, not a time machine.

"Does anyone know why? Did something happen that could have tipped them off?" Fox asked.

"I have absolutely no idea. We just returned from meeting Sacagawea then visiting with James, Ruby, and Fred when they followed us," Nellie told her father.

"Sacagawea? What was she like? I would imagine she..." Fox got excited for a moment before realizing that it was not the time to hear about the kids' visit with the Native American trail guide. "Okay, so you'd recently used The Purple Flyer. Have you checked if the radar scrambler is still working?"

Nellie and Niles shook their heads. When they first started using the time machine again after their last encounter with the agents, they'd made a point to test the radar scrambler before every flight. As time went on, however, Nellie's kidnapping felt like a distant dream and they were not as diligent about their safety. The kids believed the agents had moved on and would not bother them again.

"Well, let's go take a look at the time machine then," Fox said. He, Nellie, and Niles headed out the back door and Annie and Amelia got started cleaning up the gardening mess in the kitchen. The kids and their father quietly walked through the backyard, their minds and bodies heavy with worry. They reached the tree in the center of the yard and climbed the ladder of the tree house. There was no time to waste. If their last experience with the N.A.T. agents taught them anything, it was that they would have to work hard to protect their family.

CHAPTER FOUR

"Oh no," Niles groaned. "No, no, no, no!" His exasperation grew with every "no."

"What is it?" Fox inquired.

"The radar scrambler *is* off," Niles told him with wide eyes. "It's all my fault."

"No," Nellie interrupted. "It's *my* fault. It's my time machine. I should have been on top of this."

"While you should have been more careful, it won't do any good to place blame," Fox told them kindly. "All you can do is learn from this experience and be more careful in the future."

The kids sighed. Both Niles and Nellie were heavy with guilt. The entire family had been through so much the last time the N.A.T. Agents had investigated them. They did not want to be responsible for bringing that stress upon their home again. It was too late, however, and they knew Fox was right.

Niles made the changes needed to get the scrambler back up and running and ran a few checks to the system to be sure that it was, in fact, working again. Niles thanked him and Fox put his hand on his son's shoulder. Fox, whose red hair glowed in the setting sun, was very proud of his kids for taking responsibility and fixing the problem quickly.

They climbed down from the tree house just in time to see a familiar black town car driving slowly up towards their home. Nellie's heart began to beat faster. Niles' jaw dropped. Fox, however, inflated with rage. He'd had enough of this harassment.

He ran as quickly as he could toward the street, stepping in front of the town car as it passed their house. Riley slammed on the brakes with a terrible screech.

Fox threw his hands in the air and yelled, "Enough! You had no case a year ago and you have no case now. Leave my family alone!"

Saliva flew off his tongue as he spoke and a vein in his neck bulged.

None of the agents spoke. Riley gave Fox an angry look and swerved around him. The car picked up speed, the tires squealing as the agents quickly left the neighborhood.

Fox stood in the street seething. Annie and Amelia came out to see what the commotion was all about. Nellie and Niles stood timidly in the front yard, not knowing what to do. They'd never seen their dad so angry.

After all of the progress the Nova family made in the past year, they were right back where they started. They were terrified that something awful was just around the corner. I wish I could tell you that they were wrong, but that would be a lie. The Novas were right. The road that lay ahead of them was far from an easy one. You and I both know, however, that the Novas were very, very strong. They might have been afraid, but this time, they were ready for a fight.

CHAPTER FIVE

The next afternoon was a Tuesday. Tuesdays were always busy for the Novas because Niles had soccer practice and Nellie had both ballet and Girl Scouts. After her Girl Scout meeting, Nellie walked the two blocks to the dance studio while her dad coached Niles' soccer team. After ballet, she walked down to the soccer field, which was three blocks the other direction from dance. The Novas loved all of this activity, but it did make for slightly hectic Tuesday afternoons.

On this particular Tuesday, Nellie was in a rush as she walked to her ballet class. Girl Scouts had run a bit late because the leader handed out some newly earned badges at the end of the meeting. Nellie didn't have long before her dance class started. Her dance teacher, Miss Angela, did not take kindly to tardiness and was known to lock kids out of her classroom for being late. Nellie jogged down Main Street, trying unsuccessfully to tame her unruly blond hair and wrestle it into a neat ballet bun as she ran. At the same time, she tried to look through her backpack to find her dance shoes. As exceptional as she was, this wasn't her smartest move ever. Poor Nellie tripped on a curb and skidded down the sidewalk. The contents of her backpack went flying and scattered in every direction. It appeared as if a small library exploded on Main Street.

Nellie sighed and started scrambling to stuff every-thing back into her bag. She'd just about finished when a man stopped and picked up a thick volume on astrophysics and handed it to her. Nellie looked up, mouth open to thank him when her blood ran cold. It was agent Riley. She took off running. The dance studio was just a few doors down. Would he follow her inside? She wasn't sure, but it seemed like her safest bet. Surely, he didn't want to cause a scene in the middle of a busy studio filled with kids, parents, and dance instructors. Would he? Nellie hoped not.

She ran into the dance studio. Nellie burst into the lobby, panting and limping, and ran down the hall towards Miss Angela's classroom. Street shoes were not allowed inside the classroom, but she dared not stop to take off her shoes. She opened the door to the classroom just in time. Miss Angela locked the door right behind her as Nellie rushed in. Nellie sat down, panting and put on her ballet shoes. She saw Agent Riley peek through the window. He tried the handle. Nellie's heart stopped for a moment. Fear rushed over her and she felt paralyzed with worry.

"Parents must wait in the lobby!" Miss Angela barked. Nellie was, for once, very happy that her teacher was so stern. Riley walked away. Nellie had no way of knowing if he would stick around or not, but at least she knew she was safe for the next hour.

Nellie tried to concentrate, but I have to tell you that it's difficult to achieve perfect turn out in fifth position when you're worried about a scary government agent waiting in the lobby. Usually, the dance studio was Nellie's happy place. She found ballet class calming, tap class energizing, and jazz class so lively that she often wished she could spend even more time at the studio. Today, however, Nellie was a mess. As the class wrapped up, Miss Angela pulled her aside.

"Nellie, you seemed like you were not with us today. Is something wrong?"

Yes, a secret agent is trying to chase me down and steal my time machine! Nellie thought. *Please stop him with your high kicks and pique turns.*

Of course, that's not what she said. She could not tell her dance teacher the truth. But maybe, maybe she could use this moment to her advantage.

"It's just that I think I sprained my ankle on the walk over. I tripped and everything hurts. And I am supposed to walk over to Niles' soccer practice now. I am not so sure that I should, not with the big recital coming up," Nellie told her teacher.

It was mostly true. She tripped, there was a recital coming up, and she did not think she should risk walking to the soccer field. Her ankle, however, was fine.

"Oh, my. You should have told me! You should not dance with an injury!" Miss Angela scolded. "But you are right, you should not walk to the soccer field. Do you want me to call your mom or dad?"

"Please do," Nellie said.

Miss Angela walked Nellie to her office. She opened a small freezer next to her desk and pulled out an ice pack.

"Sit at my desk and ice your ankle while you wait for your mom to get here."

Nellie complied. Her plan had worked. Waiting in the office meant she would not be walking through the lobby. Nellie hoped that she would not be forced to encounter Agent Riley again tonight.

A few minutes later, Miss Angela popped back into the office.

"Nellie, it turns out your parents sent your uncle to pick you up. He's been waiting in the lobby for you."

"My uncle?" asked Nellie nervously.

She shook her head in disbelief. "I don't have an uncle, Miss Angela."

Miss Angela looked surprised and upset. She opened her mouth to speak, but before she could articulate her confusion, Agent Riley pushed past her.

"Hi, Honey," he said to Nellie in a too-sweet voice.

"Go away," Nellie snapped at him. "You are not my uncle!"

"Kids!" He shook his head and looked at Miss Angela. "She loves to play games with me."

Riley grinned with a fake smile that reminded Nellie of a television game show host.

"No, I don't. This man is not my uncle. In fact, he once kidnapped me and held me hostage for several hours."

Miss Angela looked very confused and uncomfortable.

"I...." she stammered. "I think I better call your mom to confirm that he can pick you up. Official policy states that parental permission has to be given before the kids leave the studio with anyone," she said, her voice trembling a bit as she came up with her excuse.

Miss Angela picked up the phone on her desk and asked Nellie for her phone number. Nellie started to answer, but Annie showed up just then.

Normally, I would say that Annie Nova had a sweet look about her. Usually, her face was warm and inviting and, upon meeting her, people frequently felt like they were talking to a long lost friend. This is not how Annie's face looked upon seeing Agent Riley. Annie looked like a mother bear, ready to attack any potential predator that may get too close to her cub.

"What...is... HE doing near my daughter?!" Annie's voice was filled with animosity.

"I... um... he said he was her uncle?" Miss Angela answered awkwardly.

"That man is NOT her uncle," Annie said angrily, her voice shaking with a rage that Nellie didn't know her mother was capable of until this very moment.

"Now, Annie. We go way back. We're practically family," Agent Riley crooned.

Annie shook her head violently. A piece of honey blonde hair fell in front of her eyes and she brushed it aside, resting her hands on her hips angrily.

"Sir, if you are not a family member of one of my dancers, I am going to have to ask you to leave or I will have to call the authorities. I don't know what is going on here, but it is clear you are no friend of this studio," Miss Angela said, trying to sound as commanding as possible.

Riley shook his head and threw his hands in the air.

"You haven't seen the last of me!" he told the Novas.

Nellie felt chillingly certain that he was right.

CHAPTER SIX

The car ride back home was silent, but the fearful whispers in Annie and Nellie's minds said more than enough to occupy the time it took to drive home. The mother and daughter were terrified. The Nova family does not scare easily, but this was serious. Riley seemed to be even more consumed with his goal to get his hands on the time machine than ever before. Nellie had the feeling that he wanted to kidnap her again, after everything that happened before. It was shocking.

Nellie's phenomenal mind spun. The inside of Nellie's mind will never cease to be a source of great amazement for me, and even in her frazzled state, this day was no exception. It was gloomy, as

it always matches her mood. A storm with tornadic winds, dark clouds, and many angry bolts of lightning whirled around at the top of the room. A sorrowful soundtrack played on floating instruments, manned by an invisible orchestra. The gigantic books flipped their pages quickly, as if feverishly searching for an answer. Whispers of conversations echoed through the room in four different languages. Giant pencils drew schematics for devices that only Nellie could truly understand, and they left a trail of purple glitter behind them as they drew.

Annie pulled the car into the driveway in front of their home. They walked absent-mindedy through the beautiful maze of a garden. As a botanist, Annie was extremely fond of plants and usually took a moment to check up on her garden on the way in and out of the house. Today, she barely glanced at the hibiscus and didn't even notice how quickly the bamboo had grown. She paused briefly, underneath the sign that read "Casa Nova" and waited for Nellie to catch up with her before entering the house.

"Nellie..." Annie's voice was filled with stress as she unlocked the door to the house. "We are going to have to tell your dad and brother everything. I know you. You are going to want to act like this wasn't a big deal. But it was."

Nellie nodded. They all knew how ruthless the agents could be. Especially Agent Riley. This was serious.

Fox and Niles sat at the kitchen table, looking at a specimen with their microscope. They were happily chattering away about cell division and did not notice that Annie and Nellie had entered the room.

Annie cleared her throat. The guys looked up, realizing that they were no longer alone. Fox smiled.

"Hi," he said excitedly. "We've just been observing cell division of some lung cells I obtained from a colleague at the university. I thought it best that the kids saw mitosis up close so that- "

"Fox. We need to talk," Annie interrupted.

A hurt expression crossed his face, but he nodded.

"Agent Riley tried to remove Nellie from the dance studio today," Annie told him. "That's the real reason she had me come pick her up."

"He what?!"

"He followed me from my Girl Scout meeting. I

think he's been trailing me," Nellie told her family.

"He must know that we allow you to walk a few blocks alone on Tuesdays. That is really concerning," Fox replied.

"What are we going to do?" Annie asked with great worry in her voice.

"I think..." Fox paused, clearly conflicted about the idea he was about to propose. "I think we should go away for a while. Hide out until they get bored of us."

"Well we can't go this moment!" Annie interjected. "You have final exams to give for end of term at the university, Niles has his soccer tournament, and Nellie has her recital. Plus, I will have to give notice to my job before I can use my time off..." Annie trailed off as she walked over to the calendar she'd tacked to the teal painted kitchen wall. "There is no way we can leave for at least a week."

Fox agreed, though he did not like the idea of waiting around Casa Nova all week. It would give the agents more opportunities to interfere with their family life, but the Novas were not the kind of people who ran out on their responsibilities. They would carefully wait a week, then head to a mountain cabin in a remote part of Washington State that belonged to Annie's mother.

Annie called Amelia to tell her what was happening. Amelia agreed to meet them at the cabin in two weeks. She would be working out of town with the airline until then.

Their plan was set. Now, all they could do was wait.

CHAPTER SEVEN

The Novas attempted to go about their week as
planned. Their home was filled with tension. Casa
Nova was normally a home brimming with so much
joy and life that it felt as if it might erupt a never-
ending stream of glee at any moment. In the days
since Agent Riley showed up at Nellie's ballet class,
the joy had been sucked right out of their home.

The kids tried to focus on their homeschool work,
but it was hard. Eventually, their parents decided it
was best to take a week off their studies and just
asked them to keep up on their reading. Nellie and
Niles both worked at college level, though Niles
had just turned twelve and Nellie was just a few
weeks short of her tenth birthday. Their parents

knew that a short break from school work would not hurt their children academically.

The Wednesday before they planned to leave for the cabin, Nellie decided it was time to read the book about Nellie Bly she'd picked up the day they'd hidden in the library to escape the agents. She brought the book up to her tree house and got started. Nellie loved to read in her tree house. Being alone with a book in a peaceful spot was Nellie's idea of perfection.

She was so impressed with Ms. Bly. Nellie found out that she was a reporter in New York City in the late 1800s. While Nellie Bly wasn't the first female reporter, she was one of just a handful at the time. Miss Bly was bold, brave and unafraid. She took on cases that no one else would. She was also full of innovative ideas that others in the journalism world hadn't thought of yet. She'd basically invented investigative reporting. Once, she pretended to be insane and spent ten days in a mad house to find out how the patients were treated. They were treated terribly, but because of Miss Bly, the city of New York stepped in and made conditions better for the patients. She also posed as a thief, an unwed mother attempting to sell a baby. The story that excited Nellie the most was when Miss Bly traveled around the world in just 72 days in an attempt to break the fictional record from the book *Around the World in 80 Days*. Nellie thought her namesake was amazing.

Before she knew it, Nellie had finished the entire book about Nellie Bly. She wanted to know more. She wanted to learn everything she could about Ms. Bly. She wanted to...

She wanted to use the Purple Flyer to meet Nellie Bly.

As strong as her desire to meet Miss Bly was, Nellie knew she wasn't supposed to use the time machine right now. Even if the radar scrambler was fixed, Fox and Annie felt that it wasn't safe. Not while Agent Riley and his crew lurked around- and were they ever lurking. The agents made it a point to be present everywhere the Novas looked. Agent Bishop stood in the parking lot of the soccer field the entire time Niles practiced one day. Another day, Fox spotted all three agents at the campus of the university when he showed up to teach a class. The agents, it seemed, were solely focused on the Nova family.

No, there would be no traveling to meet Nellie Bly. Not now.

Nellie Nova climbed sadly out of her tree house and walked slowly back toward her house. Out of the corner of her eye, she saw something black moving her direction. It was the agents, again, in their black town car. Nellie sighed in exasperation.

When will it end? she wondered. *When will it end?*

***

The week crept by. On Thursday, Fox finished his last class at the university. He asked his teaching assistant to grade the exams, so he was free to go for the summer. Friday afternoon was Niles' big game. He was thrilled when his team won 5-3. Friday was Annie's last day of work too. Now all they had to wait for was Nellie's recital.

Saturday morning, Nellie woke up early. Before she was fully awake, she knew it was a special day. It didn't fully register why it was special for a few moments. Then it hit her. It was the day of her recital! A wave of nerves and excitement washed over Nellie. She loved to dance, but the big audience at a recital always made her nervous.

The day seemed to drag on, but soon enough, the Novas made their way to the local high school where the recital was held. They were a bit worried that the agents would crash the recital, but they did not want Nellie to have to miss an important event. The agents caused enough heartache for the Nova family and they just wanted to live their lives as normally as possible before they went into hiding.

Nellie danced in three routines this year. She would perform a dance for each of the styles she studied: tap, jazz, and ballet. First up was jazz. Annie walked her backstage at the girl's dressing area with the other dancers.

"Break a leg, sweetie!" called Annie.

"Thanks, Mom!" Nellie replied cheerfully.

The dressing room was filled with happy chatter. Some of the girls giggled, a few were nervous, one tiny little girl cried because her mother would not let her put mascara on her cheeks, but everyone was excited. The feeling was palpable.

Nellie's jazz class would go on stage first, so she joined in the happy chatter and quickly dressed. She was putting on her hat when her friend, Eden whispered to her.

"Nellie! Psss Nellie!" Eden hissed.

"What?" Nellie asked.

"Isn't that the guy who tried to come into ballet class the other day?"

Nellie felt a sinking feeling in her stomach. She turned around and saw a parent volunteer trying to force a large man dressed in black out of the dressing room.

"Sir! There are little girls changing in here!" she snapped.

"I just want to give these flowers to..."

"Out!" The small redheaded woman waved her finger in the large man's face.

The door slammed shut. The woman shook her head in exasperation.

"Jazz 2! Line up!" she chirped.

It was time for Nellie to go on stage. As they walked through the hallway to get backstage, they passed Agent Riley. He winked at Nellie and whispered in a deep, throaty voice, "I'll see you after the show, dear."

Nellie's blood ran cold. But she couldn't run away. She went out on stage and danced as well as she could, but her heart wasn't in it. This wasn't just stage fright, which she did occasionally suffer from. Nellie was sick with worry over what would happen next. She turned left when she should have turned right. She stumbled and fell to the ground after a leap. At one point, Nellie just stood in the middle of the stage, not moving as her classmates danced around her. She left the stage feeling scared and embarrassed.

Nellie did not see him for the rest of the show. Her tap routine went much better than her jazz routine did, and by the time Nellie took the stage for ballet, she had almost forgotten about Riley. Nellie beamed when she met her family after the show. I am sorry to tell you that the happy moment was brought to an abrupt end. When they got to the parking lot, all three agents leaned against the Nova's car.

"He was backstage," Nellie whispered to her parents, as she pointed a trembling hand at Agent Riley.

"He what?!" Fox hissed.

"I just wanted to give these flowers to our star dancer," Riley proclaimed with a smug look on his face.

ROSES are black
Your costume was red
Give up your trick
or I'll have your head.

"I don't want your flowers!" Nellie crossed her arms in defiance.

Fox's face grew redder than his hair. He bit his lip and took a deep breath. His body shook as he tried to compose himself enough to speak. I am not sure that he'd ever been this angry in his life. A big part of being a father is protecting your family and he knew he had to do whatever he could to keep his kids safe.

"Stay. Away. From. My. Family," he seethed.

"Don't count on it," Riley laughed as the thrust the flowers at Nellie and walked away. The other agents followed.

Nellie looked down at the flowers. They were black

roses. A note was attached. It read:

"Roses are black
Your costume was red
Give up your trick
Or I'll have your head."

CHAPTER EIGHT

Annie and Fox stayed up all night packing up their belongings for their trip. They wanted to get out of the house before sunrise. They planned to be away for two full months, but not wanting the agents, who had been sitting in their parked town car down the street all week, to notice that they were getting ready to leave town, so had put off their preparations until the last minute.

They scurried about the house all night, shoving clothes, shoes, books, and other necessities into suitcases and hauling them to the car under the cover of darkness. They dared not to turn on the porch light in case the agents were watching.

Nellie and Niles did not rest well that night. Nellie

especially had a hard time falling asleep. All she could think about was the note. Was Riley that obsessed with her time machine? Would he really harm her for a chance to get it? She thought back to last year, when she was kidnapped. They eventually let her go, but the N.A.T. agents were more than willing to cross the line if they thought it would get them what they wanted. Nellie fidgeted in her bed, tossing her blankets around as if they tumbled in a dryer. The urgency of the situation took a toll on her. She was sure she'd never fall asleep, but eventually, she drifted into restless sleep filled with terrible dreams about being chased by nameless, faceless monsters in black suits.

Very early the next morning, Annie and Fox woke the children. The sky was the odd shade of purple that comes just before sunrise. They did not stop to have breakfast or change out of their pajamas. That could happen later. Now, all they needed to concentrate on was getting away.

As they climbed into the car, Niles noticed that a small trailer was hooked to the back of the vehicle.

"Hey, Dad," he said, suppressing a yawn while he buckled his seat belt. "What's with the trailer?"

Fox, who had just gotten into the driver's seat, looked around to be sure no one was near. To say he looked nervous does not begin to describe how he looked. Fox looked absolutely, positively destroyed.

"It's just supplies, Son. Coolers, lawn chairs, that kind of thing," Fox replied, anxiously.

Niles shot Nellie a look. She shrugged, too sleepy to question her father's answer.

"Let's go," Annie said, trying unsuccessfully to sound cheery.

They rode in silence. Annie originally insisting that

the kids go back to sleep, but it was clear that Nellie and Niles would not be able to get any rest. The stress and excitement of the journey ahead kept their minds too busy for sleep.

Fox had planned a route that would hopefully throw the agents off course if they attempted to follow them. Although Washington was northwest of their home state, they started off their drive by going southeast on the freeway. Fox planned to drive an entire day out of the way, stopping frequently to try to be sure they were not followed. It would make an already long trip longer, but they needed to do everything they could do stay safe.

Annie and Fox told their employers that they would be helping an ill relative in Florida. The kids told their friends the same story. The Novas were not taking any chances.

After about an hour of silence, Niles piped up from the back of the car.

"So Dad," he started cautiously. "What's really back there?" Niles pointed back toward the trailer.

Fox took a big breath in and exhaled a heavy sigh.

"It's the Purple Flyer," Fox said. "We couldn't risk leaving it behind. Now kids, just because we have it does not mean we need to use it right now. We don't know if they will be watching."

Nellie heard his words. She contemplated their meaning. But the only thought that filled her mind once he'd admitted they had the time machine was that she was going to meet Nellie Bly.

CHAPTER NINE

The Novas made four stops that day. Each time, Fox and Annie would get out of the car, walk through the parking lot of whatever restaurant or rest stop they'd found, then slowly walk through the neighborhood for twenty minutes or so, looking for signs of the agents. This might seem extreme to you, but they were desperate to protect their children. You won't understand it for many, many years, as you are young, but the instinct to keep your child safe is the strongest one we have as humans. They would do anything for those kids.

After they'd done their (very thorough) safety check, they let the kids out of the car and everyone would eat, stretch, or use the restroom. Then, the kids returned to the car and Annie and Fox would repeat their patrol. After another twenty minutes of searching the surrounding neighborhood for black town cars and men in suits, the Novas would get back on the road, changing directions at the next major highway. It was an exhausting and stressful way to travel. That night, they stayed at a hotel in a small town in Georgia. They got there well after 3:00 a.m. It was over thirty minutes from the nearest interstate but still, Annie and Fox did their long, drawn out safety check. Finally satisfied that they'd be safe, they parked the car behind the hotel and went inside and got a room. It was just before 4:00 a.m. by the the time the tired Nova family crawled into bed.

Over the next eight days, the Novas followed this same pattern. They took the most indirect route you could ever imagine as they traveled to Washington. They'd drive north for two hours, then east for one. They'd head back west for three hours, only to take a southern detour. Each time they stopped, they checked just as obsessively as the first time. They never did see a trace of the agents following them, but an uneasy feeling loomed behind them the entire journey.

Finally, nine long days after they left home, they

crossed the Idaho-Washington border. The whole family cheered. They still had several hours ahead of them, but they were relieved to at least be in the right state. By the time they made it to the cabin, it was dark. Fox and Annie performed their final safety check. All was well. When they gave the signal, Nellie and Niles burst out of the car and ran joyfully toward the cabin.

They'd arrived. Nellie couldn't help but wonder if the sense of security they felt arriving at the family cabin was a false one, however she tried to push it aside. For the next two months, this beautiful mountain cabin was their home. If they had to spend the summer in hiding, at least they got to hide out somewhere so peaceful.

Back at Casa Nova, however, the agents had just

realized the Novas were missing. Riley peeked in a living room window while Maloney and Bishop checked the back of the house.

"Any sign of them?" Riley called from the front of the house.

"No," Bishop yelled.

Maloney walked around the house, shaking his head.

"Pack your bags, boys. The N.A.T. is going on a road trip." Riley told them as Bishop made his way to the front yard.

"We'll find them if it's the last thing I do."

More than two thousand miles away, a chill shot down Nellie's spine.

CHAPTER TEN

The next morning, Nellie woke to the trilling chatter of birdsong from the forest outside. Beams of sunlight peeked into the bedroom through cracks in the curtains. She sat up in bed and stretched, taking it all in. The room was small and cheery. The walls were paneled in wood and the floors were wood as well, however a yellow printed area rug covered much of the hardwood. There was a canvas on the wall that Nellie suspected was painted by her grandmother. It was a sweet mountain scene painted in cheerful colors. Across the room was a second bed. In the bed was Niles. He was in a deep sleep, his snores filling the room.

Nellie and Niles had never shared a room before,

but they would have to learn to get along for the next few months. Nellie just hoped that Niles would not play too many practical jokes. Niles was known to play elaborate pranks on his family, but Nellie was his most common target. She was a little worried how sharing a room would impact his ability to play tricks on her, but she knew anything Niles could come up with was better than what would happen back home with the agents.

The agents. Nellie silently prayed that they would not find the cabin. She knew that her family could not hide out here forever, but she hoped that they could stay away long enough for Riley to lose interest.

The smell of bacon and eggs met Nellie's nose and she ambled to the kitchen, where she found her father standing over the stove, spatula in hand, wearing a pink and white striped apron that belonged to his mother-in-law. He smiled broadly when he saw Nellie enter the room.

"Hey kiddo! Do you want cheese on your eggs?" Fox asked.

"Yes, please," Nellie replied with a smile on her face.

For the first time in weeks, she felt calm. All of the stress back home had been a lot for a not-quite-ten-year-old to take. Soon, Annie and Niles joined them and the family took their breakfast to the deck to dine alfresco. They chatted peacefully and enjoyed the mountain air as they ate.

As breakfast wrapped up, Niles asked if he and Nellie could go exploring. Fox and Annie exchanged a nervous glance. Annie shook her head. They just were not ready to let the kids out of their sight. Not yet.

"Why don't we all go exploring together?" Annie answered.

Niles shrugged. He understood his parents' hesitance, but wasn't used to them hoovering. Normally, the Nova kids were allowed to wander their neighborhood back home alone, but normally, they didn't have to worry about being kidnapped either.

"Sure, Mom," he replied. "That would be fun."

This is how the next few days went. The Novas spent all of their time together. Fox and Annie frequently walked the perimeter of the property, checking for any signs of the agents. Nellie and Niles tried to enjoy the nature that surrounded them. It was more than a mile to the next cabin and no one was staying there this summer. Annie said it was owned by a family her parents knew and that the couple was getting on in years and didn't make a lot of trips out there anymore. It felt strange to the kids that they never saw any other people, but they knew it was for the best.

After almost a week, Niles started to get bored. Niles is a bit dangerous when he is bored, as this was when he comes up with his most elaborate pranks. He thought of some very intricate jokes, but he couldn't execute them. You see, Niles loves to use chemistry in his schemes but he didn't have access to his chemistry set up on the mountain. He was going to have to get creative.

One evening, his parents decided to barbecue some hamburgers for dinner. This is when he got his idea. He had everything he needed to prank his family all along, he just hadn't realized it. When no one was looking, Niles added some baking soda to the ketchup, closed the lid, and shook the bottle. When Fox opened the bottle a few minutes later, the chemical reaction between the baking soda and the vinegar in the ketchup created a spectacular explosion of red sticky liquid.

Niles erupted with laughter, thereby losing any

chance of feigning innocence. Fox was less than pleased with his son and ordered Niles to clean up the mess as he headed inside for a shower. Niles kept laughing the whole time he cleaned. He decided that it was worth it. Nellie wasn't so sure. She wasn't a huge fan of Niles' pranks. She did empathize with his boredom, however.

Though her days were spent hiking, drawing, reading, and swimming in a nearby lake, Nellie's thoughts were consumed with the idea of using the time machine to meet Nellie Bly. Before the mishap with the radar scrambler, the kids were allowed to use the Purple Flyer just about any time they wanted. Nellie had met so many amazing women from the past and seen such wonderful things. She missed watching out the windows to see the beautiful spiral of eternity. She wanted to talk to Niles about sneaking away to use the time machine, but their parents were rarely out of sight. She knew it would not be easy, but that didn't stop her from trying to come up with a plan.

Nellie's most magnificent mind was in overdrive, trying to hatch a plan that would allow her to freely travel through time again. The ballerinas whipped round and round in dizzying fouetté turns. The pages of the giant books flipped feverishly. The invisible orchestra played an upbeat, hopeful song. An eagle soared above the towering wall of gears. The gears below slid around, changing positions to create something new. Suddenly, a bell chimed somewhere near the giant pencils and Nellie knew how she would make it all happen.

That evening, while the rest of the cabin slept, Nellie carefully and quietly crawled out of her bed and made her way across the room. She poked Niles, who momentarily stopped snoring, let out a grunt, and rolled over. She sighed and tried again. Niles flailed his hands around in front of his face.

"Niles," Nellie whispered loudly.

Niles let out a confused grunt.

She sighed again. "NILES," she hissed as she shook his shoulders.

"Huh? What are you doing?" he queried.

"We've got to talk," she told him.

Niles sat up, rubbed his eyes, and looked at the digital clock on his nightstand. "Nellie, it's 3:35 in the morning. Can't it wait?" he moaned in protest. "Ssshh," she scolded. "You'll wake Mom and Dad. And no, it can't wait. The fact that it's

the middle of the night is precisely why this conversation must happen now. It's the only time that Mom and Dad aren't hovering."

"What's going on?" he asked quietly.

"I can't stand this," she told him. "We never go anywhere, we're never alone. I'm bored. I know you are, too. Plus, I really, really want to use the Purple Flyer."

"I get that Nellie, but Mom and Dad have every reason to be nervous," Niles replied.

"I know. But we fixed the radar scrambling issue. I

know they are scared. I am too, but I can't stand life like this."

"Well, even if we wanted to, we couldn't. Not with Mom and Dad always watching," Niles responded.

"They're not watching *now*."

Niles' eyes widened. Nellie was not the kind of kid who usually disobeyed her parents.

"You want to go right now?" he asked.

"Not tonight. The day after tomorrow. I want to go on my birthday. Are you in?"

A most mischievous grin filled Niles' face as he nodded eagerly.

They had a plan.

CHAPTER ELEVEN

The day of Nellie's tenth birthday, her parents decided that they could leave the property and drive into the nearest town to get pizza. Fox and Annie didn't want to let the recent stress caused by the N.A.T. agents ruin Nellie's birthday. Normally, the Nova's made an enormous fuss over birthdays. They threw elaborate parties with lots of friends, some sort of hired entertainment like a magician or a DJ, and all of the yummy food a kid could ever want. They felt bad for Nellie and wanted to do what they could to make up for the lack of party.

At 5:00 that evening, the Novas piled into their car and headed down the mountain. When they arrived in town, Fox stopped the car a few blocks from the restaurant. He parked in front of a bank and he and Annie got out of the car and walked around the area for about twenty minutes to ensure they hadn't been found. Nellie and Niles sat in the car, tummies rumbling while they waited. Fox and Annie declared the area to be free of N.A.T. agents, so they drove on toward dinner. Once they parked, Fox and Annie walked the parking lot just once before allowing the kids to follow them into the restaurant.

The family walked into the pizzeria and the pleasant aromas of pepperoni and garlic bread welcomed them. It was a small restaurant, but the cheery yellow walls and faux-Italian decor put the family at ease. Though the Novas had never been there, the restaurant felt familiar and inviting, as if they'd been there a thousand times before. Fox pointed out a table in the back and told the kids to sit down while he and Annie ordered. Nellie nervously smoothed out the checkered table cloth.

A moment later, a bell chimed to indicate that the front door of the restaurant opened. Nellie and Niles instinctively looked up. For a fraction of a second, Nellie feared the agents found them, but instead of three men in black walking through the door, it was just one woman. A woman they were

elated to see, Amelia Earhart.

"Auntie Amelia!!" the kids cheered as they bolted from the table toward the front of the restaurant. After a few minutes of hugging and excited chatter, everyone found their way back to the table. The five of them were relieved to be together again and the kids very much enjoyed being surprised by Amelia's arrival. A waiter brought two large pizzas to their table and everyone ate with much enthusiasm.

Though this birthday party was the simplest she'd ever had, Nellie knew her parents worked hard to make the day special, and they'd succeeded. She appreciated the gesture and momentarily reconsidered her plan for evening. Nellie Nova was not the kind of kid who made elaborate plans to go against her parents' wishes. As she sat at the table of the pizzeria, enjoying her slice of pepperoni, she wondered if she'd made a horrible decision. Her guilt grew stronger when they presented her with her gift, a new microscope with a screen and a camera so she could save images of the specimens she studied. Her parents knew her so well!

She spent the entire car ride back to the cabin feeling awful. Could she really lie to her parents? Things only got worse when she got home. It turned out that Annie had secretly baked a beautiful three layer chocolate cake frosted with elaborate fondant flowers for her the night before. The cake tasted even better than it looked. Nellie felt sick to her stomach with guilt, but in the end, her desire for adventure was just too strong and she reluctantly decided to stick to her idea.

After they had cake, Amelia had another surprise in store for the kids. She walked them down the trail to the lake and pointed out a seaplane. The plane floated on the lake next to a dock.

"I thought we could take a quick flight to celebrate Nellie's birthday," she said.

"Can we? Please?!" Nellie begged, looking hopefully at her parents.

Annie and Fox smiled.

"Yes, we've already discussed it. Happy birthday, sweetie!"

"Yay!" Nellie squealed with delight.

"Woohoo!" cheered Niles.

Both kids looked as if they might burst with excitement. The kids broke out into a sprint. They ran to the dock and bounced impatiently while the adults walked toward the plane. Annie let out a laugh.

"I haven't seen you kids this happy since we got here."

"I don't think we have been!" Nellie answered.

They all climbed into the plane and Amelia started it up. They took a tour of the wilderness from above. It was so beautiful from this vantage point. They could see nothing but mountains, trees, and miles and miles of wilderness. The sun began to set as they made their descent back on the lake. It was such an enjoyable flight that Nellie almost forgot her plans for later that night. Almost.

That night, she and Niles got out of bed just before midnight, as Nellie wanted her adventure to actually take place on her birthday. They carefully and quietly put on their shoes, tiptoed out of their room, down the hall and out the backdoor. They slowly made their way to the shed behind the house where Fox stored the time machine. Nellie tried the handle. The shed was locked. She groaned in frustration.

"What?" Niles whispered.

"It's locked. I should have known! Where does Dad keep the key?"

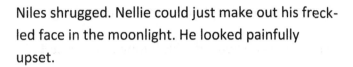

Niles shrugged. Nellie could just make out his freckled face in the moonlight. He looked painfully upset.

He's just a frustrated as I am that we can't use the time machine, Nellie thought.

Just then there was a rustling in the bushes behind them. The hair on Nellie's back stood up.

"Did you hear that?" Nellie whispered to Niles.

"Hear what?" Niles held still and listened.

It was silent for a moment and he shrugged. But Nellie didn't feel right about it. Niles started walking around the shed, looking for another way in. Nellie scanned the darkness, looking for a hint of whatever made that sound.

"Maybe this window?" Niles quietly suggested, pointing to a small window on the side of the shed.

He tried the window unsuccessfully. He let out a frustrated sigh and walked to the back side of the shed. Nellie still felt uncomfortable. Something wasn't right. She was sure they weren't alone.

"Niles," she whispered with a hint of panic in her voice. "Niles, come back."

She heard the rustling again as he came back to the front of the shed.

"Did you hear it this time?"

Niles nodded. He looked sickeningly frightened.

The sound grew louder and the kids knew that whatever was making it was getting closer. Nellie grabbed her brother's hand and braced herself for whatever was coming. Three adult figures burst through the bushes. Niles gasped. Nellie let out a terrified scream.

They'd been found.

CHAPTER TWELVE

The largest figure reached for Nellie. A terrifying, shrill noise filled her ears. It wasn't until she felt the vibrations in her throat that she realized that her fear was involuntarily leaving her body through a scream.

"Nellie! It's okay!" Niles told her.

Just then a bit of moonlight passed onto the figure's face. It wasn't, as she feared, Agent Riley. It was Fox, looking quite shocked.

"Oh! Dad!" she gasped, her heart beating wildly in her chest.

"What are you doing out here?" Annie said from behind Fox.

"It's just the kids?" Amelia asked in surprise.

Nellie sighed. Now that she wasn't scared, she was frustrated. She was so close to getting to use the Purple Flyer again. Now that the adults found them, she'd lost all hope of that happening.

"We were going to use the time machine," she told them. "I really wanted to meet Nellie Bly. And I thought it would be so fun to do it on my birthday. I know I was wrong for going behind your back. I'm sorry."

Fox looked at Annie, hopefully. Annie shook her head no.

"Let's go inside, kids," Fox said.

The short walk back to the cabin felt like an eternity to Nellie. Niles, too, felt heavy as he walked. The kids didn't get into trouble often, but they didn't often do anything that required discipline. Their parents had always been fair, but the Nova kids' minds were filling with possible punishments.

Amelia excused herself to her bedroom. Fox and Annie told the kids to sit down at the kitchen table. The room was filled with tension. Niles wiggled in his seat, as he often did when he was nervous. Nellie looked at her feet, not wanting to meet her parents' eyes.

"I have to tell you that we're disappointed in you two. We've discussed this before. You are not to travel in time without talking to us about it," Annie said with an exasperated tone.

"You really should have talked to us," Fox added.

"I know it was wrong. It's just been so difficult to be cooped up in this cabin. It was inconsiderate of me to try to do this without permission," Nellie told them.

"And I was wrong to go along with it," said Niles.

"Please understand that we empathize with you. It isn't easy hiding out all summer, being away from your friends and unable to use the time machine for so long," Annie said with her usual warmth filling her voice.

Fox nodded. "No one's enjoyed this."

"But you can't do this. You can't get up in the middle of the night and just leave," Annie added.

Nellie and Niles nodded.

"If you would like to use the time machine, you will have to get our approval. Every single time," Annie said.

Nellie's heart beat a little faster.

"You mean we can use it?" She asked, trying not to be too hopeful.

Annie looked to Fox. He nodded.

"We have no reason to believe that we are being watched here. We've had no contact from the agents since we arrived. So, yes. You can. WITH approval. And you MUST check the radar scrambler before leaving. Every single time you use it. No matter what,"Annie insisted.

Nellie and Niles jumped out of their seats with excitement.

"But you are not going anywhere in the middle of the night," Fox added. "You will need to be well rested so you can think clearly and make good choices."

"Can we go in the morning?" Niles asked

"Please?" Nellie pleaded.

"After breakfast," Annie told them.

The kids cheered. Fox and Annie sent them to bed.

Not that it did much good. Nellie and Niles didn't do much sleeping. They stayed up whispering with excitement about the adventures that lay ahead of them.

CHAPTER THIRTEEN

Though the kids thought they would never fall asleep, eventually they did. Before they knew it, the morning greeted them by warming their faces with beams of sunshine. Niles woke first, lying in bed for a few minutes, his mind groggy and his eyes heavy. Before Niles had fully roused, Nellie woke up.

Nellie's mind instantly knew she had a reason to get out of bed. *The time machine. Nellie Bly. Adventure.*

Nellie bounded out of bed and ordered her brother to do the same. The sooner they got up and ate breakfast, the sooner they'd be in the Purple Flyer, heading toward Nellie Bly.

Nellie had created a plan to intercept Miss Bly on her round-the-world trip. The first stop would be Hoboken, New Jersey, where Miss Bly's journey began on the ocean liner *Augusta Victoria* in November of 1889. Nellie wanted to see her namesake at the start of her exciting voyage. Nellie was wondering if she would be able to get a chance to speak to Miss Bly at a crowded dock when her mother interrupted her train of thought.

"Nellie, Niles?" called Annie cheerfully from the kitchen.

"Yes, Mom?" Niles answered.

"Come sit down and eat breakfast. You've got a big day ahead of you and I don't want you time traveling on an empty stomach."

Nellie and Niles exchanged a glance and giggled. Sometimes, even though they were used to time travel by now, talking about it just sounded ridiculous. They walked into the kitchen and found their parents and Amelia sitting at the table with an unreasonably large quantity of food surrounding them. Fox and Annie loved to cook together, but this was a bit much, even for them.

A plate in the center of the table was heaping with

sausage and bacon. Next to it, a bright teal bowl was filled with blueberry muffins. Beside the muffins sat a large dish of scrambled eggs and next to that was a plate full of croissants. A silver platter held an assortment of donuts. A pink patterned bowl held strawberries, blueberries, grapes, and raspberries and at each place setting was a large glass holding a smoothie. There was so much food at the table that it was almost comical.

"So, you've been cooking then?" Nellie asked playfully.

"We just want you two to get a good start to your day," Annie answered with a smile.

The kids wolfed down a large amount of food in

record time. Annie insisted they take some muffins and croissants with them so they would have a snack if they needed it, but Nellie felt certain that she would not want to eat again any time soon, whether she was in 2016 or 1889.

After lots of hugs and warnings to be safe, the kids headed out to the shed.

It was time.

CHAPTER FOURTEEN

I am fairly certain that Nellie Nova had not been this excited since her very first time traveling excursion. The longer she waited to use the Purple Flyer, the more her anticipation grew. Nellie loved time travel more than anything she'd ever done and waiting had been immensely difficult for her to endure. Though she tried not to let her face show just how thrilled she was, Niles knew. When he saw Nellie's face as they entered the shed and saw the time machine, he let out a little giggle.

"You're really ready for this, aren't you?" he chuckled.

"I've waited too long! Let the adventure

commence," she replied.

She opened the door to the time machine and Niles followed. She stored the bag of snacks her mother insisted they take in a hinged bench and pulled out some 1800s-inspired clothing for them to wear on their travels. She thrust a pair of knee length pants called knickerbockers at Niles as well as a brown wool jacket, tie and white button up shirt. Nellie and Niles turned away from one another and changed, Nellie putting on a blue bodice and a full, knee-length skirt over a bustle. In the year the Novas had been traveling in time, Nellie amassed quite a collection of historical clothing.

Niles was not especially pleased with his new look. He sighed and parted his fire-red hair to the side. He was not a fan of dressing up, but they both knew that they would fit in much better in 1889 with these clothes than if they'd worn their jeans and t-shirts. Nellie attempted to calm her curls, but they would not comply. She quickly gave up and her sea of blond hair seemed to rebel, looking wilder than ever.

"Oh well," she said with a sigh. "I don't want to bother with fixing my hair when we could be on our way to 1889!"

She walked over to the control panel and entered their destination: November 14, 1889, Hoboken. New Jersey, USA.

She looked at Niles with a joyful smile. The music inside her amazing mind increased its tempo and played a happy tune.

"Are you ready?" she asked.

"So very ready!" he replied.

Nellie pulled a lever and the machine began to spin. The kids didn't realize that they'd made a terrible mistake. They had not checked the radar scrambler. Their thoughts were elsewhere as green

light filled the time machine and soon, it lifted off the ground and into eternity, spiraling as it moved. The kids watched out the window in a state of wonder. It did not matter how many times they used the time machine, they were always amazed by the journey through time. They gasped as a civil war army rushed forward into the stars. A moment later, they jumped as a monkey swung past the window of the time machine on a vine and then swayed off into some eternal rain forest. As the monkey flew out of sight, a group of school children cheered as a bell rang in a one room school house and they ran excitedly out the door. The machine began to descend as they saw a pirate ship sailing on the stars.

"Brace yourself," Niles said with a smile.

The rate of spinning increased and the machine moved rapidly toward the ground. The kids waited for the jarring landing they knew was coming. They touched down with a bounce and the Nova kids cheered with glee.

They'd arrived.

CHAPTER FIFTEEN

"Welcome to the year 1889. You are in Hoboken, New Jersey. The local language is English. Do you need more information?" chirped the Purple Flyer.

"No thank you!" Nellie answered quickly. Her heart swelled with gleeful anticipation. After weeks of being unable to use her time machine, it was finally time to meet the woman she admired so much.

"You ready?" she asked Niles as she rushed to the door.

Niles nodded, his freckled face covered with his ever-memorable mischievous smile.

"Let's go!"

The kids burst out of the door of the Purple Flyer and found themselves in a small park. Nellie ordered the Purple Flyer to turn on its invisibility shield and they headed off into the city. Nellie had already mapped out their route to the pier, which was only about half a mile away.

Though it was not their first time traveling in the past, the Nova kids were overcome with a feeling of wonderment. A lot had changed in 127 years and Nellie and Niles took in every detail with great pleasure. They walked excitedly down the cobble-stone streets, whispering about the clothes, the buildings, and the horse-drawn carriages moving quickly by them, hooves clattering on the bumpy roadway. Nellie loved this part of time travel. It was like stepping into another world.

As they approached the docks, the kids noticed that quite a few people were gathered there. Nellie worried that it would be hard to spot Miss Bly in this crowd. The *Augusta Victoria* leaving port drew a large crowd, and Nellie Bly's trip added to the excitement in the air.

"I'm starting to think I didn't plan this out very well," Nellie told her brother.

Niles nodded, scanning the crowd, hoping to catch

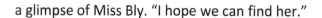

a glimpse of Miss Bly. "I hope we can find her."

Just then, Nellie saw her, about 150 yards away. She'd seen photos of Miss Bly in her cap and checkered coat in books, so she was easy to spot near the ramp to the ship talking with a few men, presumably her newspaper colleagues.

"Niles!" she squealed. "Niles she's right there!"

Niles gave Nellie a high-five and they worked their way toward Miss Bly. The crowd was thick and the kids had a hard time weaving their way around people, most of them adults who didn't seem to notice the frantic-looking children.

Just when they'd almost reached Miss Bly, a man rushed by them, accidentally knocking Nellie over with his trunk. He looked over his shoulder and shouted a quick apology as he ran up the ramp. Niles helped Nellie up. When they looked back to where Miss Bly had been standing, she was gone.

Nellie sighed with disappointment. Niles tried to comfort her, but he really wasn't good at such things. He awkwardly patted her back, then pulled his hand off of her as if he'd been caught with his hand in a cookie jar. The Nova kids were getting along better than ever, but like many twelve-year-

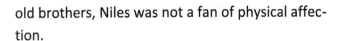
old brothers, Niles was not a fan of physical affection.

"Where did she go?" Niles asked, feeling helpless.

"I don't know," Nellie replied, depressed to have come so far just to lose track of her hero.

The kids watched as the last few passengers got on board and the crew prepared the ship for its voyage. As the ship pulled away from the dock, Nellie spotted Miss Bly on the passenger deck. She nudged Niles with her elbow. Nellie couldn't be positive, but it appeared that Miss Bly made eye contact with her. Then, Miss Bly winked. And just as quickly as she'd been spotted, she moved away and was lost in the crowd of excited passengers.

"Did you see that, Niles? She winked at us!" Nellie squealed.

"I think so!" Niles nodded enthusiastically.

The kids made their way back to the Purple Flyer, trying not to be too disappointed that they didn't get a chance to talk to Nellie Bly. Nellie was already chattering away about different times they could interact with her on her round-the-world trip. She was debating where they should go next when Niles reminded her that they'd promised their

parents that they would check back in after each destination in time they visited.

Nellie was frustrated, but she knew that he was right. They'd have to head back to the cabin in 2016 before they could do anything else. They walked in silence until they reached the Purple Flyer and Nellie ordered its invisibility shield to deactivate.

The kids got into the time machine. Nellie told the Purple Flyer the location of the mountain cabin and the kids began their amazing journey through time. Though her heart was a bit heavy because she'd missed out on Miss Bly, Nellie felt better as she watched time spiral around her.

I'm a lucky kid to get to experience all of this beauty, Nellie thought as she watched a herd of wild horses run free on a heavenly plain.

The Purple Flyer landed with a bump. The kids left the time machine with their spirits lifted again.

CHAPTER SIXTEEN

Nellie and Niles landed back in 2016 with a thump. They ran into the house about two minutes after they'd originally left.

"Hi!" Nellie shouted.

Fox, Annie, and Amelia met the kids at the kitchen table.

"How'd it go?" asked Annie curiously. Fox stood behind his wife. He was barely able to contain his excitement. Unable to hold still, he was tapping his foot and smiling broadly.

"Well. We saw her. But just barely," Nellie said, her disappointment resurfacing as she spoke.

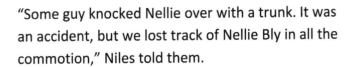

"Some guy knocked Nellie over with a trunk. It was an accident, but we lost track of Nellie Bly in all the commotion," Niles told them.

"I'm fine," Nellie insisted before her parents had time to ask.

"I'm sorry you didn't get to talk to her, kiddo," Fox said, pushing Nellie's wild curls out of her face as he spoke.

"It's okay. I am working on another plan so we can see her again. I wanted to intercept her on multiple points on her trip. Can you believe she made it around the world in seventy-two days in 1889 and 1890? It's crazy. Anyway, I think if we show up earlier this time, giving a full hour at the train station she departed from in France, we'll have a better chance for interaction," Nellie said. She turned to Niles.

"What do you say? Want to grab lunch and then head out?"

Niles nodded enthusiastically. It may have still been morning in 2016, but he was hungry. They'd spent three hours in 1889.

"Wait, you want to leave again today?" Annie asked nervously.

"Yeah! Please, Mom. I missed my chance. I need to try again." Nellie pleaded.

"Annie, I think we should let them," Fox said. "There's no real reason to make them wait another day."

Annie sighed and looked at Fox, then at Amelia. She saw the look in both sets of eyes- they wanted this adventure as much as the kids did.

"Fine," she relented, "You can go, but only if we get some healthy food in you before you go." She was, after all, a mother, and even mothers of time travelers insist that their kids eat before leaving the house. I don't mean to embarrass Nellie and Niles, but she also made it habit to remind them to use the restroom before they left, much their chagrin.

Two turkey sandwiches on whole grain bread later, the kids gave everyone a hug and ran out the door toward the shed. They were happily chatting about all of the adventures that lay before them as they walked. They were so very excited about what was to come next. So excited, that I must tell you, they missed something very important. They didn't notice that three men in black suits stood in the forest, watching them. The Nova kids didn't notice that when they went into the shed, the agents walked toward the house, and they had no way of knowing that when they started up the Purple Flyer, Agent Riley broke down the front door of the cabin and the agents rushed in on a shocked Annie, Fox, and Amelia.

The kids didn't know that while they spiraled toward 1889, their world was crashing down around them in 2016.

CHAPTER SEVENTEEN

Back in 2016, Fox, Amelia, and Annie sat down at the kitchen table after saying goodbye to the kids. Annie picked up her cup of coffee and took a slow sip. Fox looked wistfully out the window, his eyes telling the stories of the expeditions through the ages that he longed to take. Amelia, who was especially antsy, knowing that she was to be stuck in the cabin for quite some time, let out a long sigh.

"Well. Now what?" Fox asked. He turned away from the window and looked at the women sitting at the table with him.

"I was thinking we could go on a hike when the kids get back. I don't want to leave now, because they always time their return for so close to when they leave," Annie said.

Before anyone could respond to her suggestion, the door burst open.

Back already?" Fox called out toward the front of the cabin.

The agents barged through the small cabin, following the sound of Fox's voice. Annie let out a gasp as they stepped into the room.

"Did you miss me?" Agent Riley asked wickedly.

***

Back on the Purple Flyer, the kids had no clue what their parents and Amelia were going through. They thoroughly enjoyed the maze-like beauty that is eternity. Nellie let out a happy sigh as they watched hundreds of butterflies flutter over a field of flowers. Niles giggled when a moment later, they saw bear cubs wrestling playfully in an ethereal forest. They braced themselves as the time machine began its decent toward Earth in 1889.

The time machine landed with its usual bump and the kids stood up and looked out the window to take in their surroundings. Nellie's face was filled

Nellie Nova's Summer on the Run

with a gigantic smile. Her grin was infectious; upon seeing her face, Niles couldn't stop himself from smiling just as broadly.

"Welcome to Amiens, France. The year is 1889. The local language is French. Do you require more information?" chirped the Purple Flyer.

"No thank you," Nellie responded.

She turned toward Niles. "Shall we go?" she said in her best imitation of a French accent.

"We shall!" he responded.

I've mentioned that the Nova kids were gifted in many ways. They were brilliant scientists, excellent mathematicians, and budding historians. I'm sorry to say, however, that the ability to correctly mimic an accent was not a gift either child possessed and they sounded quite silly. Quite silly indeed.

Feeling as though they might burst from excitement, the kids turned off the invisibility shield and stepped into the chilly French night. They set off to find Nellie Bly.

***

"What are you doing in my house?" Fox demanded of the N.A.T. agents in 2016.

101

"You know very well what we're doing here," snarled Riley, who, as usual, had made himself spokesman for the agents.

"I really don't know. We're just trying to enjoy a family vacation and you can't leave us alone. It's getting ridiculous how obsessed you are with my family. Now leave, or I will call local law enforcement," Fox said, trying to sound braver than he felt.

Riley let out a sick laugh that let everyone in the room know that he was not afraid of the local police in the least. The agents by his side joined in his laughter, though Bishop's laugh wasn't convincing. It was clear that he was uncomfortable.

The cozy cabin suddenly seemed claustrophobic and gloomy. The Novas and Amelia had nowhere to hide. It felt like they were in a lot of trouble, and I am so sorry to tell you this, but they were. They were in a whole lot of trouble.

***

Niles and Nellie wandered around the train station, listening to bits of conversation. Both kids spoke French, which was useful for eavesdropping in a foreign land. No one was really saying anything all

that exciting, but they hoped they'd hear something about Miss Bly. They didn't. Nellie knew that
Miss Bly was currently meeting with Jules Verne,
the author of *Around the World in 80 Days*, the
book that had inspired Miss Bly to journey around
the world unaccompanied. Nellie imagined that the
two of them were having an amazing conversation.

She and Niles blended in as best they could, trying
not to draw attention to themselves. They enjoyed
people-watching in just about any time period. The
kids were so happy in 1889 that they could never
imagine the terror their loved ones were experi-
encing in 2016.

***

Fox's heart pounded violently as if trying to escape
his chest. He had to find a way out of this. But
how? How could they get away? His eyes met
Annie's and he knew she was searching for a way
out as well. He turned toward Amelia and the look
on her face that indicated she might just have an
idea. Fox decided his best bet was to distract the
agents so that Amelia could execute her plan.

"I've grown tired of our visits," Fox told the agents
with great disdain in his voice. "I wish that I had
created a time machine, but I truly have not. You

have been relentless. You even kidnapped my daughter, for goodness sake, and you have found nothing. It's time for you to give up this silly idea and quit harassing my family!"

Agent Riley laughed again. "Maloney." He barked to the agent on his left, "Get the handcuffs!"

Fox glanced nervously at Amelia, hoping she had been given enough time to find them a way out. She turned away from him, Annie and the agents, facing the window. Before anyone realized what she was doing, she leapt out of the open window and Fox and Annie quickly followed.

It was fairly high, about seven feet up, but not so high that they'd risked serious injury. Still their adult knees were in shock after a jump like that, but adrenaline kept them going.

"To the lake!" Amelia hissed as the agents scrambled to follow them through the window.

Off they ran, toward the lake, praying that they could find a way out of this mess.

***

"Niles!" Nellie said excitedly. "Niles, look! It's her!" Nellie Bly was making her way toward the train at a

quick pace. She wore a checkered jacket and a cap on her head. She carried only one small bag. Miss Bly, you see, had a point to prove. Her editors told her that it would be impossible for a woman to make a trip around the world because she would require "dozens of trunks" on a long trip. Miss Bly's single bag was only sixteen by seven inches.

"All aboard for Brindisi, Italy!" called a man.

Miss Bly quickened her pace. Nellie and Niles broke out into a run to try and catch her.

"Miss Bly! Miss Bly!" Nellie called desperately.

Nellie Bly paused, turned and saw the kids behind

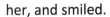

her, and smiled.

"Miss Bly, can I just have a second of your time?" Nellie asked.

"I have only a moment," Nellie Bly told her. "My train is boarding."

"I just wanted to tell you that I think you're amazing, traveling the world all alone," Nellie told her.

"Well, thank you!" Miss Bly said. "What's your name?"

Nellie blushed. "It's Nellie! Just like you! But I know Nellie is a pen name for you. But it's the name my parents gave me! And this is Niles," she said, pointing to her brother. Nellie had a habit of rambling nervously.

"Well, you seem like a spunky kid. I bet that you'll do something amazing one day, too!" she smiled at the kids and then said, "I'm sorry, but I have to go catch my train. I've got a fictional record to break, you know!"

With that, she was off, running quickly toward the platform. Nellie let out a happy squeak. Niles poked her and laughed. It always cracked him up, how excited she got when she met someone she

admired.

"Well, let's go home," he said.

They walked back to the Purple Flyer. Nellie was silent, but her mind was full of excitement. The invisible musicians played lively tune.

Back in the time machine, the kids changed their clothes in anticipation of their return home. After pulling on her jeans, Nellie had an idea.

"What if we didn't go home yet? What if we met her back in New Jersey on the day of her return? Just to get one more glimpse of her trip around the world?"

"But Mom and Dad..." Niles began.

"Mom and Dad won't notice the difference until after we are back," Nellie insisted. "Dad said there was no reason we had to wait a day in between traveling in time."

She'd convinced him. They headed back to the time machine delighted with their plan to head to New Jersey in 1890. They wouldn't have been so cheerful if they knew what awaited them in 2016.

CHAPTER EIGHTEEN

As Nellie entered their destination into the Purple Flyer's computer, her parents and Amelia ran desperately through the forest. As Niles and Nellie watched the beautiful display of time out the window of the time machine, Fox tripped, rolling twenty feet downhill. As the time machine landed with a bump in Jersey City, New Jersey, Annie and Amelia struggled to help Fox to his feet. As Nellie and Niles exited the time machine and turned on the invisibility shield, they had no idea of the horrifying danger their parents faced.

The kids eagerly made their way to the train station. Nellie knew that the station would be crowded as Miss Bly's fans waited to meet her upon her historic arrival, so they got to the station

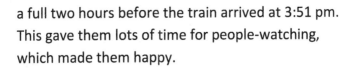
a full two hours before the train arrived at 3:51 pm. This gave them lots of time for people-watching, which made them happy.

When the train arrived, the reaction of the crowd was deafening. America loved Nellie Bly, and there she stood, waving her cap and smiling at the station-full of people. Nellie's heart sank as she worried that she would not get a chance to speak to Miss Bly. She let go of her disappointment, realizing that she and Niles were lucky just to be at the station as Miss Bly arrived. Nellie thought about all the places Miss Bly had visited and briefly wondering if they should catch up to her again in Hong Kong or Italy. She looked at her brother and smiled. They cheered along with the crowd, their addition to the colossal roar of applause.

After several minutes, police officers helped Nellie Bly make her way through the sea of people. Nellie wriggled her way closer, desperate for just one more moment of conversation with her. Niles hurried to keep pace with his sister, feeling frustrated at having to keep an eye on her and at the same time admiring her for her tenacity.

"Miss Bly! Miss Bly!" Nellie called out as she walked past. Nellie jumped up and down, waving her arms around. Niles stood by her side with a sheepish grin

on his face.

Why, in all the commotion, Nellie Bly noticed Nellie Nova's calls, I can't explain, but she did. She stopped and turned around toward the Nellie and Niles. Her face lit up with recognition.

"Don't I know you kids? From France?" The Nova kids nodded enthusiastically.

"We're Americans, we just vacationed in France. We like to travel." Nellie told her namesake.

"Why, I daresay you're as plucky as I am," Miss Bly exclaimed and she took the cap off her own head and set it on Nellie's. "I have a feeling that you two are full of adventures. Maybe one day, you'll make it around the world, too!"

And with that, she was gone, swallowed by the monstrous crowd.

It took the kids quite some time to make their way out of the train station and back to the time machine, but they were in no hurry. When you can travel in time, you don't feel the need to rush to make it home.

While they walked along, talking happily about their day, their parents sprinted through the woods toward the lake. While they entered the location of the cabin into the computer, the agents got closer and closer to catching Fox, Annie, and Amelia. While the kids enjoyed their journey through time and space, a hand reached for Annie's shoulder. The exact moment the kids landed in 2016, Annie let out a bloodcurdling scream. Riley had caught up with her.

CHAPTER NINETEEN

"Did you hear something?" Niles asked his sister as the time machine landed. "I swear I heard a scream."

"It's probably just a mountain lion," Nellie answered, unworried.

Niles nodded in agreement, but a heavy wave of dread washed over his body. He could not shake the feeling that something was very, very wrong. He was, of course, correct. Niles often was. This was a time that he was hoping to be wrong.

The kids quickly changed back into their normal clothes, turned on the invisibility shield, and headed toward the house. They didn't make it inside before they knew something was wrong. The window to the kitchen was open and they could see from the outside that chairs had been over-turned inside.

"I don't think that was a mountain lion, Nellie," Niles whispered.

She shook her head. "I don't believe it was."

"What do we do?" Niles asked his sister.

"We have to find Mom, Dad, and Amelia," she answered. "And we can't get caught."

"The N.A.T. agents? How did they find us?" Niles asked, his eyes wide. "We checked. Didn't we check the radar scrambler?"

"I don't know, Niles," Nellie answered with as reas-suring a tone as she could muster, "But we can't worry about that now. For now, our only focus needs to be finding our family."

Niles nodded, but his nerves got the best of him. His stomach felt like it was filled with tiny, back--flipping ninjas and his whole body tingled. It was impossible to think. He hoped that Nellie would be able to figure out how to find their parents.

Nellie was worried, but her amazing mind kicked

into high gear. The dancers turned rapidly in time to an unnerving song. The enormous books' pages flipped so quickly that they made a whooshing sound. Fear filled her mind and the usually bright light dimmed. Suddenly, a giant light bulb lit and Nellie knew what to do.

"We need to track them. Remember when I was working on my *Naturalist* badge for Girl Scouts?"

Niles nodded. "Well, I decided to take some books out from the library to learn more about the outdoors. And I kind of went on a tangent with my reading and ended up reading about tracking. First, the book talked about tracking animals, but it said the same concepts could be used with humans. We need to look for signs of where they've been."

"Okay," Niles began, "But how?"

"We need to look for disturbances on the ground," Nellie said. She scanned the ground around the front of the house, brushing her wild hair out of her eyes to get a better view.

"Okay, see this?" She pointed to some upturned dirt on the ground. Niles came over to check it out. The brother and sister knelt down on the ground to inspect it further.

"It looks like three people ran through this soil," she said.

"So was it Mom, Dad, and Amelia? Or Riley and his cronies?" Niles asked, staring at the indentations on the ground.

"It's hard to say, the prints are not perfect," she answered thoughtfully.

"I can tell they were running because the prints are deeper on the toes than the heels and they are pretty far apart. Hmm. I think these might be the agents' tracks, because they are all fairly large. If they belonged to Mom, Dad, and Amelia, two would be significantly smaller because women's

feet are more petite than men's."

"Okay, so we know the agents went that way," Niles said, pointing to a trail.

Nellie nodded. "And likely, they were chasing Mom, Dad, and Amelia, so...." she gulped.

"We have to follow the agents if we want to help our family," Niles finished.

Nellie nodded again, and without a word, the kids hurried off down the path as fast as their feet would carry them.

CHAPTER TWENTY

The kids raced wildly through the forest, silently praying that they'd reach their parents and Amelia before they were harmed in any way. A sinking feeling overwhelmed Nellie as they ran. She knew that they had to help her parents, but she did not know how. The pitter-patter of her pounding feet taunted her. *Think-think. Think-think. Think-think,* they seemed to say as she ran faster and faster toward danger.

Suddenly, there was no time left to think. She heard another scream and she could tell its source was nearby. Nellie tapped Niles' shoulder and held up her hand to indicate they should stop. When he did, she held a finger to her lips, quietly shushing

him. They stopped and listened.

"You're not going to get away!" Riley growled.

"We don't have a time machine!" Fox insisted.

"You keep saying that, but I don't believe you!" Riley replied.
"You've torn up our home, kidnapped our daughter, ransacked my office, and made an enormous mess of our cabin. Where exactly do you think this time machine is?" Fox hissed at him, clearly seething with anger.

"Niles," Nellie whispered, "We have to move the time machine."

"But they need our help now!"

"I know, but if the agents find the time machine, we'll all be in trouble. You go back to the shed. Move the machine deep into the woods. You know the clearing with the daisies by the pond?"

Niles nodded, remembering the spot from a hike they'd taken about a week ago.

"I will figure out how to get us out of here some- how," she said with determination in her voice. "We will meet you there as soon as we can," she told him.

He gave her a quick hug and ran off toward the cabin. Nellie inched closer to the lake shore, where her parents and Amelia were being held. They were still arguing with the agents about the existence of the time machine.

Nellie decided to create a distraction, hoping that one or more of the adults could escape if the agents were looking away from them. But what could she do?

Nellie inched her way closer, stopping when she was about ten feet away to take in the scene in front of her. Amelia was closest and she was facing toward the forest. Nellie stared at her, willing her to take notice. After a moment, Amelia's eyes widened. She'd seen Nellie. Amelia's eyes darted toward the dock, about three-hundred yards down the lake. It took Nellie a moment to figure out what she was trying to tell her, but next to the dock was Amelia's seaplane. Amelia already had an escape plan! Nellie just had to figure out how to set it into motion.

Still not exactly sure what she was doing, Nellie picked up a small gray stone from the forest floor. She held it in her hand, trying to decide what her next move was. She didn't want the agents to notice the plane before the she, her parents, and Amelia could reach it.

She took a deep breath and threw the stone into the lake in the opposite direction of the seaplane. It hit the lake with a loud splash.

"What's going on over there?" Bishop wondered aloud.

Nellie crawled on the ground toward the seaplane, staying behind the tree line. Bishop, who'd been holding Amelia, let her go so he could investigate. Nellie and Amelia made eye contact again, knowing this was their chance. Nellie slowly stood up, then threw another rock. The second splash caught the

attention of the other agents, who then walked
Annie and Fox over toward the shore with them.
Amelia and Nellie would have to figure out how to
save them later, for now, they needed to run!

They worked their way toward the dock, quietly
creeping until they'd put one-hundred yards
between themselves and the agents, then broke
into a sprint. Amelia's absence went unnoticed.

Amelia and Nellie silently walked down the dock,
afraid that so much as a breath would alert the
agents to their location. Once at the plane, they
carefully climbed the ladder, opened the door, and
rushed to the cockpit. Amelia started the plane.
The roar of the engine caught the attention of the
agents who now realized that they'd lost a hostage.
Amelia pointed the plane toward the agents, Fox,
and Annie. It moved along the water quickly.

Fox and Annie knew that they had precious little
time to act. Fox kicked Agent Riley square in the
stomach. Riley fell to the ground in pain. Agent
Bishop rushed over to Riley's side. Maloney tight-
ened his grip on Annie. The plane sped at them as
fast as Amelia could maneuver it. Annie tried to
fight her way out of Maloney's arms, but failed. She
scratched, kicked, and screamed, all without result.
Fox ran toward her. She bit down on Maloney's

arm at the same time Fox reached them and kicked his knee. Finally, his grip loosened and the couple ran toward the plane.

"We're going to have to jump onto the pontoons as the plane goes by!" Annie shouted to Fox as the sound of the plane overwhelmed them.

He nodded and the two held hands and waded into the lake. A moment later, it was time. Amelia slowed as much as she could, but hoped they would know what to do. They did. Fox and Annie each took hold of a pontoon. This was not an easy task as the plane moved quickly on the surface of the water. They pulled themselves up onto the pontoons, carefully moved toward the ladder, and climbed into the open door, while Amelia maneuvered the plane away from the agents. Riley scrambled to his feet, jumped into the lake, desperately grabbing at the pontoons, but he was too late. Amelia picked up speed and the plane took off.

They'd escaped.

CHAPTER TWENTY-ONE

Nellie rushed frantically to the back of the plane as her parents scrambled through the door. Fox slammed it behind him. His face was ghostly pale. Annie didn't look any better.

"Where is Niles?" she asked Nellie, trying unsuccessfully to hide the fear in her voice. She was worried in a way that only a parent can worry about their child. Not knowing if your child is safe or not is about as terrible as it gets for a parent.

"He's fine, Mom," Nellie said reassuringly. "I had him take the Purple Flyer to the clearing by the pond," Nellie answered.

A rush of relief washed over Annie's face.

"Amelia," Fox called to their pilot, "Head east. Niles is by the pond."

"No problem," she said as she changed the plane's direction. Within a few minutes, they could see the pond and the clearing, but no sign of Niles. The plane filled with tension as Amelia landed the plane on the water.

"Where is he? He said he'd be here!" Nellie wondered aloud.

Nellie, Amelia, Fox, and Annie got off the plane and waded through a few inches of water to get to the shore. They stood next to the pond for a moment, fraught with worry for Niles. Water dripped off Fox and Annie's clothes.

"What do we do?" Annie asked with tears in her eyes.

Before anyone could answer, they heard some rustling in the woods near the clearing.

The agents! thought Nellie. She could feel her heartbeat pounding in her head. *How did they get here so quickly?*

They all turned toward the rustling, and much to their relief, saw Niles coming out of the bushes.

"Niles!" Nellie called and ran to her brother, throwing her arms around him.

After a few minutes of hugging and catching one another up on what had happened, all five of them went silent. They were safe, but only for the moment. The gravity of the situation weighed heavily on them all.

"What now?" Fox asked no one in particular.

"We can't go back to the cabin. Or go home," Annie said.

"And we can't stick around here for long," Amelia

added.

"Right," Fox said. He turned and took in his surroundings. His eyes darted around as he scanned the forest to be sure the agents had not yet caught up to them.

"Niles, show me where you left the Purple Flyer. We've got to load it onto the plane and get out of here."

Niles nodded and the two redheads headed a few meters into the woods. A few moments later, they popped back into the clearing and rolled the time machine toward the plane. Nellie, Annie, and Amelia waded through the water and got back into the aircraft.

After Fox and Niles finished loading the time machine, they all buckled up and Amelia started the plane. They watched out the windows as they flew away from the pond, passing the lake and the cabin. The sweet little cabin looked like a doll's house from this vantage point. Nellie felt her heart sink a bit knowing they wouldn't return.

After a few moments, Amelia spoke up.

"So where *are* we going?" she asked no one in particular.

"I think," answered Nellie, looking back toward the Purple Flyer, "that a better question is *when* are we going?"

A silent agreement was made between the five of them in that moment. There was nodding of heads, but no one spoke. It was understood. They were leaving 2016. The Novas and Amelia flew on in silence, knowing that their lives were about to be changed in ways they didn't dare imagine. They were in for a most amazing adventure.

But that's a story for another day.

THE END

ABOUT THE AUTHOR

Semi-nomadic, Stephenie and her family currently live near Raleigh, North Carolina. Her kids are Texans at heart. (Hi, McKinney!) Steph and her husband grew up outside of Seattle. (What up, Port Orchard?!) Stephenie writes, creates art, and homeschools her three amazing kids. Stephenie likes to hike with her family and drink lots and lots of coffee.

This is Stephenie's second book.

You can find out more about the author and her family at www.stepheniepeterson.com.

If you or your child enjoyed this book, please take a moment to leave a review on www.amazon.com or www.goodreads.com.